R○

○CHOOL

You're thinking about doughnuts

IT WAS COLD, spooky and very boring.

Frank hated Friday nights, sitting in the
museum while his mum did the cleaning.
He felt very alone . . . until a skeleton
came over for a chat.

'How about a doughnut?' asked the skeleton.
'OK.' said Frank.

And suddenly the museum didn't seem quite
so boring any more.

But after a few chilling encounters with some of
the skeleton's weird and wonderful friends,
all Frank really wants is his mum . . .

You're thinking about doughnuts

—

Michael Rosen

ILLUSTRATED BY SARAH TISDALL

—

BARN OWL BOOKS

First published in Great Britain 1987 by
André Deutsch Children's Books
Scholastic Publications Ltd
Commonwealth House, 1-19 New Oxford Street
London WC1A 1NU
This edition first published 1999 by Barn Owl Books
157 Fortis Green Road, London N10 3LX

ISBN 1 903015 03 0
A CIP catalogue record for this book
is available from the British Library

Designed and typeset by Douglas Martin
Printed in China

Chapter One

FRANK said he didn't want to go but Mum said he had to.

'Can't I stay here on my own?' he said.

Mum shouted at him, 'Why do we always have this nonsense? I can't leave you with your nan every Friday, can I? And I can't leave an eight year old boy on his own in the house for three hours of an evening.'

'I want to stay here,' said Frank.

'You're not listening to me, are you? You're coming, and that's that.'

Frank knew the 'that's that' business. There was never any getting round Mum when she came out with the 'that's that'. He sat there saying, 'that's that' to himself without making a sound and at the same time pulling a funny face. 'That's that', 'that's that'. Luckily for him, Mum didn't see. She was busy putting her overall in her bag and pinning up her hair.

'Can I bring my cars?' said Frank.

'What happened last time you brought your cars?' said Mum.

Frank looked very hard at the ground and tried not to laugh.

'Yes, you may laugh, Frank, but it wasn't you that

put your foot on one of those cars and went flying down the corridor at ninety miles an hour, was it?'

Frank remembered Mum doing just that.

'I could've broken my neck. Can you imagine? Me in hospital? My friends coming to see me, saying, 'How did it happen, love?' and I say, 'I had a car accident.' 'Oh dear,' they say, 'Were you in the car, or were you run over?' 'No,' I say, 'I was *on* the car. I put my foot on it.'

Frank listened. Sometimes she was funny when she was cross, he thought.

'Bring a comic or something, will you? I don't think you'll be able to break my neck with the *Beano*, will you?'

Frank nipped upstairs and dug out an ancient comic without a cover from under his bed, and next thing, Frank and Mum were off. It was six o'clock, dark and raining. They were going to work. Mum was a cleaner. Every Friday night she went down town to do three hours cleaning at the City Museum. Frank hated it. He had to sit on a hard wooden bench and wait. The light was always dim, the heating was always off and Mum would disappear off down a corridor or up some stairs and he'd be all alone in this great big echoey place for hours and hours. All he'd see was the rows and rows of glass cases and the shiny floor. Sometimes he had nightmares about it. Once he dreamt about the stuffed tiger on the stairs. It had run at him. His whole dream was this huge tiger run-

ning at him, and roaring and biting his face. He could see right down its throat and watch the great teeth snapping at him just a few inches away from his eyes. It was horrible.

But there was nothing he could do about this evening. Friday night was museum night. And 'that's that', said Frank to himself.

3

Chapter Two

THE MUSEUM. Up the steps. The big grey stones in the walls. The pillars. The statues, all those stone people.

'Blimey,' thought Frank, 'one of them winked. That one at the end. The one with the beard and the sword, with no clothes on. He winked. I saw him.'

'Mum,' said Frank, 'who's that?'

'Him?' said Mum, looking at the naked man with the sword, 'that's your uncle Charlie.'

'No, really, Mum,' said Frank. 'Who is it?'

'How should I know?' said Mum. 'All I know is that he shouldn't go waving that sword about without his trousers on. Now come on, Frank.' She had the key in her hand. Frank looked at the statue again. Maybe it didn't wink.

As soon as they were in the museum, Mum got her overall on and sat Frank down on the bench.

'Now listen here. You stay put right here, Frank. You don't move. You don't walk off. You understand me?'

'Ye-e-e-e-e-es, Mum,' said Frank.

She looked at him as if to say, 'Don't you be such a cheeky worm,' but she said nothing and off she

4

went past the glass-cases and out of sight. It made him feel rotten all over to see her go. He wanted her to come back even if it was only to shout at him for being cheeky or stupid.

He was all on his own. The great big hall. Empty. No one else there. The shiny floor. The high roof. Looking up at those little windows, high up. Scarey to think of someone cleaning them. Frank saw himself like an acrobat in the circus leaping from one of the windows over to one of the huge lights that dangled down from the ceiling. 'Oh no,' he daydreamed, 'I've missed. I'm falling. I'm falling. I'm falling.'

Then everything went quiet.

Everything was very quiet.

Frank felt very alone.

Then he felt his eyes move very slowly sideways.

They stopped when they got to a glass case on the other side of the hall. He was looking at a big human skeleton. As he looked, the skeleton seemed to bend very slowly forwards. Frank felt his hands go hot. The skeleton's hand seemed to fiddle with something in one corner of its glass case. He heard a rattling. He swallowed and the noise in his throat swelled in his ears. The skeleton opened the front of the glass case. It did. He saw it. Then it stepped out on to the shiny museum floor and began to walk. Frank didn't move. It was walking towards him. He couldn't move. A great white skeleton was walking slowly across the shiny floor towards him. All Frank dared do was

stare. But it was unbearable to watch it walking nearer and nearer. Finally, it arrived at Frank's bench and
stood over him.

Frank looked up and into the dark holes where the
eyes should be.

It spoke to him:

'Well?'

'What?' said Frank in a little squeaky voice.

6

'Well,' it said, 'what do you want?'

'I don't want anything,' said Frank.

'You must want something,' said the skeleton. 'Everyone wants something. I've never heard of anyone who didn't want anything at all.'

Frank just stared at it.

'You're boggling,' it said. 'You're just boggling. You're not even thinking what I asked you. What's the matter with you? Don't you listen when people ask you things? Stop boggling and listen. What do you want?'

'Nothing,' said Frank.

'Look here, we've done that one already. Don't waste my time, boy. I proved that you must want something, because everybody does. If you say you don't want anything, you must be lying. I don't like people who lie.'

Frank thought about it. He didn't think he was a liar.

'I know what you're thinking,' said the skeleton, 'You're thinking you're not a liar. Look here, just tell me something you want.'

Frank looked blank.

'How about a doughnut. Do you want a doughnut?'

Frank thought about doughnuts. 'OK,' he said, 'yeah, I want a doughnut.'

'There you are,' said the skeleton. 'You do want something.'

Frank felt very puzzled. He also felt hungry. Well, hungry enough to eat a doughnut.

'I know what you're thinking,' said the skeleton. 'You're thinking you weren't hungry until I started talking about doughnuts. But now I've said "Dough-nut!", you want a doughnut, don't you?'

Frank nodded.

'And I'll tell you something else. I haven't got a doughnut to give you. And what do you think of that, eh?'

Frank muttered a 'nothing' to himself. He was feeling a bit silly by now.

The skeleton said, 'Do you know why I asked you what you want?'

'No,' said Frank, 'I don't.'

'Oh come on. It's obvious.'

'No, I don't know,' said Frank.

'Because I want you to ask me what I want.'

'Do you?' said Frank.

'Yes,' said the skeleton.

Frank looked at it again.

'Well, come on then, for goodness sake. Ask me what I want.'

'What do you want?' said Frank in a wooden voice.

'I want to be real.'

Frank had no idea what it was talking about. Did it mean it wanted to be human and have flesh and blood?

'I know what you're thinking,' said the skeleton, 'you're thinking it's time I gave you a doughnut.'

Frank said, 'No I wasn't. I was wondering if you wanted to be alive again.'

'What do you mean, "again",' said the skeleton. 'I never was alive. That's the whole point.'

'Do you mean you were always dead?' said Frank.

'Oh come on, boy, come on. Have you ever heard of anyone who was always dead?'

'No.'

'Well, there you are then.'

'But then,' said Frank, 'I haven't heard of a skeleton talking.'

'I am not a skeleton, OK?' said the skeleton.

'What are you then?'

'Thank goodness you asked, boy. I thought you'd never ask me. Look. I'm made of plastic. I'm a model. I'm a replica. I'm a copy. I am not real. Do you understand?'

'Oh,' said Frank in a small voice.

The plastic skeleton slumped down on the bench beside Frank. 'It's no good. I'm just a great big plastic idiot skeleton.'

Frank thought for a moment, and wondered if it should be telling him all this but then he said, 'Look, I hope you don't mind me asking this, but what are you doing in this place if you're not real?'

'I know, I know,' said the skeleton. 'Exactly. What *am* I doing in this place? I could be in all sorts of other places. I could be in a school, couldn't I? Helping people learn how all this stuff works.' At that the plastic skeleton bent its arm backwards and forwards. 'I know how to do it, you know. I even know all the names. Do you know what this one is, boy?'

'It's your arm, isn't it?'

'No, no, no. The name of the bone, you fool.'

'It's your arm bone.'

'No. It's the humerus. The humerus. You say it.'

'The humerus.'

'There you are. You see, you've learnt something. I know what you're thinking now. You're wondering how we can get back to talking about doughnuts.'

'No I wasn't,' said Frank. 'I'm still wondering what you're doing here.'

'Right, yes,' said the plastic skeleton. 'Listen,' it whispered, looking over its shoulder. 'I'm a copy of the wild man of Ashton Forest. You've never heard of him, have you?'

'No,' said Frank.

'Follow me.' It took Frank over to the glass case it had just climbed out of. 'Look at that.' It pointed to a sign in the case that said:

'For years, the wild man roamed through Ashton Forest, terrifying children, threatening farmers and killing cattle, until finally it died in 1886. This is a plastic copy of the original skeleton.'

'One day,' said the plastic skeleton, 'I'm going to

find the real wild man of Ashton Forest's skeleton and I'm going to tell him that he can get in that smelly glass case instead of me and he can sit there day after day, night after night and have people staring at him. I'm fed up with it. He can have a go.'

The plastic wild man of Ashton Forest's skeleton got up. 'And then I can take up ballet dancing, I've always wanted to be a ballet dancer.'

It stopped. 'I know what you're thinking,' it said. 'You're thinking when am I going to ask you what you're doing here?'

'No, I wasn't thinking that', said Frank. 'I was wondering whether you've got any doughnuts.'

'No I haven't' said the plastic skeleton, 'but I think I know where there are some. Shall we go and have a look?'

'Yeah,' said Frank.

'Right, let's go. And anyway, why are you here?'

'I'm waiting for my mum.'

'Don't be silly,' said the plastic skeleton. 'No one waits for their mum. They look for their mum. No one waits. No one waits.'

'Look,' said Frank, 'I'm waiting for my mum, OK?'

'No, you're not. You're looking for her. I can see you are. You keep looking round and looking up the stairs. You're looking for her, aren't you?'

'I suppose I am,' said Frank.

'There you are,' said the plastic skeleton. 'I'm always right. Now what we're going to do is we're going to look for doughnuts. And I'll tell you something else. We're going to look for the real wild man of Ashton Forest's skeleton, as well.'

'Are we?' said Frank in that small voice. 'Is he here?'

'Of course he is, you doughnut,' said the plastic skeleton.

'I'm not a doughnut,' said Frank.

'Aren't you?' said the plastic skeleton.

Suddenly, Frank started feeling worried again. Perhaps this skeleton thought people like him were doughnuts and it was going to eat him. And were they really going to look for the wild man of Ashton Forest's skeleton?

'Right, we haven't got long,' said the plastic skeleton. 'Let's go. We've got lots to do: doughnuts, the wild man, doughnuts and the wild man.'

And the two of them, the plastic skeleton and Frank, began to cross the shiny museum floor together.

Frank was beginning to think that looking for his mum would be a good idea as well.

Chapter Three

'EXCUSE ME,' said Frank, 'can I ask you a question?' 'Go ahead,' said the plastic skeleton, as he strode across the shiny floor.

'Who is the man outside made of stone?'

'Which man?' said the plastic skeleton, 'There are hundreds of them. The man who built this place loved statues, so he built hundreds of them.'

'The man with the beard and the sword and no clothes on.'

'They're all men with beards and no clothes on. That's the whole point. There's a whole army of them out there. They're Greeks or Romans, I'm not sure which. Anyway, they're all mad.'

'How do you know?'

'Because they come in here, don't they? And drive us all mad, with their shouting and singing and waving their swords about.'

'How do they get in?'

'When people leave the side door open, that's how. Straightaway, they're off their walls and pillars, they're through the door and next thing there is a heap of them fighting and hacking at each other in the middle of the museum. They're mad. No, they're worse than mad. They're dangerous. That's because they attack anything they see. They scream horrible things and come running at you. Some of them have got lances and daggers instead of swords. Your mother didn't leave the door open tonight, did she? Sometimes she . . .'

Frank felt funny. He couldn't remember. Did she?

'You've got me worried now,' said the plastic skeleton. 'Quick, let's get down to that door and see.'

The pair of them rushed back to the side door where Frank and his mother had come in. But it was too late. Just as they came round the edge of the cloakroom they heard some shouting and doors rattling.

'Oh no,' said the plastic skeleton, 'they're coming. Quick, dive down here.' And they ducked down below the level of the counter in the cloakroom.

'They're not even real, you know,' whispered the plastic skeleton.

'I know that,' said Frank, 'they're made of stone.'

'No, you doughnut, what I mean is that they're not real Greeks or Romans. They're not thousands of years old. They just look like that. They're only about a hundred years old. They're just English blokes dressed up as Greeks. They're only pretending.'

As the plastic skeleton said that, Frank could hear something that sounded like people coming out of a football match. There was chanting and clapping and singing and laughing. Suddenly, the door burst open and a great stream of these men with beards and

14

swords and no clothes on came rushing through. They were singing something that sounded like, 'We are the champions, we are the champions.' But it was, 'We are the stonemen, we are the stonemen. Easy. Easy.' Then there was clapping. Then someone else started going, 'Stat-stat-stat-statUES, stat-stat-stat-stat-UES.' More cheering, then some booing. One group started singing: 'Oh when the stones come marching in, oh when the stones come marching in . . .' That started some of the others banging their swords and lances on the shiny floor. DUM DUM DUM-DUM-DUM. DUM DUM DUM-DUM-DUM. 'Oh the city stone men sing this song, doo dah, doo dah. Oh the city stone men sing this song, doo dah, doo dah day.' There now seemed to be hundreds of them spilling into the museum. The noise was deafening. Suddenly one of them shouted, 'R-U-U-U-U-U-M-BLE', and next thing they were at each other's throats; fighting and kicking and hacking away at each other for all their worth. Frank turned his eyes away. He couldn't face looking at them. He was sure someone was going to get very badly hurt or even killed.

The plastic skeleton whispered in his ear: 'Don't be stupid, boy. They can't hurt each other. They're made of stone.'

Frank giggled.

'Sshhhh,' said the skeleton, 'but they can hurt *you*. *You're* not made of stone, are you?'

Too late. Frank had been heard by one of the men.

He heard a great roar that sounded like a mixture between a motor bike and an elephant and all of a sudden there was one of the statues standing on the counter right above his head.

'Hey fellers,' he said, 'look who wild man's brought with him.'

The mention of the name 'wild man' soon got some of the others going. Frank heard shouting: 'Wild man, wild man, what a load of rubbish!' Someone started singing to the tune of John Brown's Body something like:

'The wild man's bones are plastic right through,
The wild man's bones are plastic right through,
The wild man's bones are plastic right through,
*   but we go marching* ON ON ON. *'*

More cheering.

The plastic skeleton was grabbed by two of them and then next thing Frank himself was dragged out from under the counter as well. The pair of them were hauled out into the middle of the museum. Some of the statues didn't take much notice but just went on fighting and hacking and biting and pulling, but there was a group of about twenty or more who were jeering and shouting at Frank and the plastic skeleton. Frank was feeling very, very scared. The swords were waving about right near his face and he felt his arms being held really tightly, so tightly in fact, it

16

hurt.

One of the stone men stuck his face right into Frank's and yelled, 'Who are you, son?'

Frank said, 'I'm Frank.'

'Well, Frank,' he shouted, 'do you know who I am?'

'No,' said Frank.

'I'm Hercules, OK?'

Then another one put his big stone face into Frank's face and yelled, 'And I'm Mars, God of War, me you know.'

Soon they were all shouting their names out and

prancing about showing off their muscles and waving their swords about.

'I'm Achilles,' says one.

'So? I'm Zeus, King of the Gods.'

'I'm Jason, boss of the Argonauts.'

'I'm Neptune.'

One after another they shouted their names out. Then that set off another one of their shouting chants: 'We are the heroes, we are the heroes.' More cheering and clapping and banging of swords on the floor: DUM DUM DUM-DUM-DUM. DUM DUM DUM-DUM-DUM.

Then one of the stonemen, who said he was called Pluto, got them all to be quiet.

'Right, quiet, you lot, quiet. Shuttup a minute, will you? The thing is, what are we going to do with them, now we've gott'em?'

'Yeah,' shouted Mars, 'what are we going to do with'em?'

'I know,' said Zeus, 'let's tie 'em up and throw things at them.'

'Yeah,' said Theseus, 'we could go and break open a few cases and find stuff to throw at them.'

Mars rushed over to one of the glass cases nearby. Frank just had time to glance into it. It was full of big jugs and bowls and things.

'Oh no,' Frank heard the plastic skeleton saying, 'that's the African stuff.'

Zeus was jumping up and down grinning. 'Chuck

18

it at them, chuck it at them.'

'Stop it, stop it,' shouted the plastic skeleton. 'All those bowls and things have got to go back to Nigeria.'

'They aren't Nigerian,' shouted Hercules, 'so how can they go back to Nigeria? They belong to General Fawcett, wild man.'

The moment Hercules said the name, 'General Fawcett,' all the stone men started cheering: 'Gen'ral Faw-cett, Gen'ral Faw-cett.' And then they sang: 'There's only one General Fawcett . . .' and they chanted 'General Fawcett walks on water.' More cheering and clapping.

The plastic skeleton had time to mutter to Frank, 'He came back from Nigeria, this Fawcett man, a hundred years ago, same time as these stone men were made. They love him.'

'Why?' said Frank.

'Because he killed lots of people.'

'What?' said Frank.

'And because he brought back treasure.'

'What treasure?' said Frank.

'The treasure that belonged to the people he killed, of course.'

'Where is it then?' said Frank.

'A little bit of it is in that glass case Mars has just broken, but no one knows where the rest of it is.'

Frank looked at Mars and he had cracked the side of the glass case where all the bowls and jugs and

things were. The stone men were cheering and slap‑
ping each other's backs. Zeus stuck his face between
the plastic skeleton and Frank and shouted 'Shuttup'
amazingly loudly at them.

Frank was feeling scared. Two stone men still had
hold of him by the arms and it was hurting.

Just then Hercules jabbed his sword through the
glass case where the African bowls were and glass fell
all over the floor. More cheering. Then chanting:
'Chuck it, chuck it, chuck it.'

At the same time, some of the stone men who had
been shouting, 'There's only one General Fawcett,'
were over by another glass case and they were shout‑
ing something else: 'The medal, the medal, the me‑
dal,' and then another sword went through that glass
case, with glass all over the floor.

Neptune grabbed hold of some army medals out
of the case. This caused riot and excitement. They
started waving the medals about, shouting, 'We've
got the medals, we've got the medals. We are invinci‑
ble. We are invincible.'

'They're General Fawcett's medals,' said the plas‑
tic skeleton. 'Queen Victoria gave them to him.'

'Why?' said Frank.

'For killing people of course. Don't you know
anything, boy?' '

'SHUTUUUUUUP,' yelled Zeus.

Jason and some of the Argonauts now got hold of
some of the African bowls. Frank thought. 'That's a

bit of General Fawcett's treasure, is it? I wonder where the rest is.'

'Chuck it, chuck it, chuck it,' shouted the stone men.

Frank got ready to protect his face, the plastic skeleton turned its skull away as the stone men got ready to throw. Frank was terrified.

Just then, something very strange happened. High up, above the hall where all this was going on, there was a kind of gangplank, that came out of an attic door. The attic door opened and out on to the gangplank walked a woman in a long dark dress. Her voice sounded out above the din. 'And what do you think you're doing?'

It was a very posh voice.

Immediately, the noise stopped. The stone men were hushing each other up. Swords were dropped, the banging stopped. The cheering died away. Everything went very still.

'Never, in all my life,' said the woman, 'have I ever seen such goings on. You, Neptune; you Zeus – what do you think you were doing? Mars, I am disgusted. Nothing to say for yourselves? Suddenly lost our tongues, have we? Well, I am appalled. Every single one of you, you should be ashamed of yourselves. Thoroughly ashamed. I am lost for words. Just look at the mess. Jason, aren't you supposed to be in charge of the Argonauts? I cannot believe that you, of all people, could behave so badly. I am so disappointed in every single one of you. What a way of going on!'

The stone men stood there, with their heads hanging, looking sulky and sheepish.

'Well, listen here,' she went on, 'I don't want to know who started this. I want this place cleaned up, tidied up and absolutely spotless by the time I come back. Do you hear me? Now jump to it. Every one of you.' The moment she finished speaking, she turned round and walked briskly back down the gangplank, through the attic door and back into the attic.

Right away, the stone men set to work getting everything cleaned up. They didn't shout or cheer or stamp or clap. They did the whole thing whispering.

They let go of Frank and the plastic skeleton and didn't seem to take any notice of them.

'Who was that woman?' said Frank.

'That's Mrs Longstone,' said the plastic skeleton.

'Who's Mrs Longstone?' said Frank.

'Mr Longstone's wife,' said the skeleton.

'Who's Mr Longstone?' said Frank.

'Mrs Longstone's husband,' said the plastic skeleton.

Frank had run out of ways of asking who this person was, so he stood and watched the stone men clearing up. Everything was going back into its proper places. They were even mending the glass cases so that all the pieces of glass were being put back and all the cracks in the glass were disappearing. The stone men looked like different people. They seemed like brilliant workmen who could make their stone hands do whatever they wanted. In a flash, the whole place looked absolutely spick and span as if no one had touched it.

Neptune came over to the pair of them: Frank and the plastic skeleton. He muttered, 'Look I'm really sorry about all this. I don't want to make excuses but we've been stuck out there on the wall and the pillars for weeks and weeks now and I suppose we ... er ... just got carried away or something.'

The others heard what Neptune was saying and thought that maybe he was saying sorry for all of them, so they just hung their heads or nodded and filed out one after the other: Theseus, Hercules, Zeus, Jason and the Argonauts, Achilles – all of them. They shut the door behind them and Frank and the plastic skeleton of the wild man of Ashton Forest were left once again standing on the shiny museum floor.

Chapter Four

'I KNOW what you're thinking,' said the plastic skeleton.

'What?' said Frank.

'You want your walnuts.'

'What walnuts?' said Frank.

'The walnuts you were thinking about,' said the plastic skeleton.

'We weren't talking about walnuts,' said Frank, 'We were talking about doughnuts.'

'No,' said the plastic skeleton, 'we were talking about walnuts.'

'Well,' said Frank, 'I wasn't thinking about walnuts or doughnuts, OK? Maybe *you* were thinking about walnuts.'

'Don't be silly,' said the skeleton, 'I never think of walnuts. All right, what *were* you thinking about, boy?'

'I was wondering where my mum is.'

'Is your mum Mrs Longstone?' said the plastic skeleton.

'No,' said Frank, 'of course she isn't.'

Now Frank was puzzled. He thought the plastic skeleton knew who Mrs Longstone was. He didn't know everything.

'Look,' said the plastic skeleton, 'we haven't got much time. I want to find the real wild man of Ashton Forest.'

'I thought you wanted to find some doughnuts first,' said Frank.

'Aha,' said the plastic skeleton, 'you were thinking about doughnuts. I knew it, boy. I knew it. You can't hide anything from me, young man.'

'Oh blow these rotten doughnuts,' thought Frank, 'I don't even like doughnuts very much.' But as the plastic skeleton seemed like his only friend in this place, he said, 'All right, yes, I was thinking about doughnuts, really.' This seemed to please the plastic skeleton.

By now, they had walked across the shiny floor of the museum and had got to the bit marked MODERN. Just then Frank saw, out of the corner of his eye, something move. He looked, but all he could see was the exhibit of the Moon Probe and the Space Shuttle. There was the lunar module and next to it stood an astronaut.

As Frank looked at it, he heard a voice. It was an American voice and it sounded all crackly with lots of hissing behind it, just like a voice on a bad radio. It was talking a bit like Neil Armstrong, the first man on the moon; the man who'd said, 'That's one small step for a man, one giant leap for mankind,' when he put his foot down on the moon.

'Hi,' said the astronaut, 'hi, guys. That's one small step for a man, one giant leap for Popeye. It looks like a beautiful little place we've got there. Hi. Hi, guys. That's one small step for a man, one giant leap for peanut butter sandwiches. Hi. Hi.'

Frank looked at the plastic skeleton. 'Aren't you going to say, "hallo"?' said Frank.

'We don't say hallo to him, he might want a conversation,' said the plastic skeleton.

'Look,' said Frank, 'he's waving.'

'Oh no,' said the plastic skeleton, 'he saw you looking friendly.'

'Hi,' said the astronaut again, 'you guys need some sleep. Can you debug this thing?'

'He's walking towards us now,' said Frank.

They watched as the astronaut walked nearer and nearer. Finally, he got to them and put one arm round Frank and the other round the plastic skeleton.

'Hi, hi, guys. How big is space? What is it like in space? What is space? Where is the earth in space? Huh?'

Frank was looking right into the window of the space suit just where the astronaut's head ought to be and there was nothing. Nothing at all. It was just a space suit with nobody inside it.

So then Frank said to it, 'What question do you want me to answer first?'

'Hi, hi, guys. That's one small step for a man, one giant leap for the Wizard of Oz.'

'Don't take any notice of him,' said the plastic skeleton.

But Frank was really interested. After all, this was the first time he'd met an astronaut. Except this wasn't an astronaut. Well, he thought, it was the first time he'd met a space suit. So Frank said, 'Did you go to the moon?'

'Of course he didn't,' said the plastic skeleton, 'he just walked about outside.'

'Outside what?' said Frank.

'Outside the space craft, you know, the Space Shuttup.'

'The Shuttle, you mean,' said Frank.

'That's what I said,' said the plastic skeleton.

So Frank tried again. 'Why did you walk outside the shuttle?'

'It's no use asking him questions. He's not allowed

to answer anything.'

'Why not?' said Frank.

'Because it's secret.'

'What's secret?'

'Everything's secret.'

'No, it isn't,' said Frank, 'I know that Apollo went to the moon. That isn't a secret.'

'No, no, no. Everything you don't know about, is secret.'

'Why?' said Frank.

'In case you find out, of course,' said the plastic skeleton.

'Find out what?' said Frank.

'How do I know?' said the plastic skeleton. 'If I knew I'd tell you, but I don't know because he's never told me.'

The space suit started up again: 'Hi, hi, guys. Is it difficult to keep fit in space? Is weightlessness harmful? How do spacecraft land? What are G-forces?'

'How much do you get paid for this?' said Frank, staring in through the window. 'I'll ask it some questions,' he thought. 'Never mind what the plastic skeleton says. How much does your space suit cost? Do you wish you were in Star Wars? Did you meet any Russians when you were up there? Are you going to have Star Wars up there with the Russians?'

Then Frank stopped. He stopped because the space suit seemed to have heard Frank's questions and was now waving its arms about and jigging up and down.

'You've made him angry now, you fool,' said the plastic skeleton. 'You've asked him all the questions he's not supposed to answer.'

Next thing, the space suit was jumping back to the lunar module and space shuttle exhibit. When it got there, it went straight for the models of the rockets: Apollo, Venturer, Voyager and the shuttle itself. Then it started throwing them. It picked them up like darts and started throwing them at Frank. One after the other, these model rockets came flying through the air at him. He ducked and dodged and managed to get out of the way of most of them. One of them hit his arm, though, and it hurt.

'He really likes doing that,' said the plastic skeleton.

Frank was scared that it had all got so dangerous. 'This is like the stone men again,' he said.

The plastic skeleton thought that was a joke and laughed.

Then as soon as the space suit had thrown all the rockets it started jumping towards them again. Frank got ready to run away.

'Hi, hi, guys. Will man ever reach the planets? What lies beyond the stars? That's one small step for a man, one giant leap for cheese crackers.'

'Ask him quick,' said the plastic skeleton.

'What?' said Frank.

'One of the questions he keeps asking you.'

'Oh,' said Frank, '. . . er what lies beyond the solar system?'

'Vast regions of space that are empty except for traces of gas,' said the space suit, 'then many millions and millions of miles further on lie the stars of the Milky Way. The Milky Way and the solar system are part of our galaxy. Beyond our galaxy lie other galaxies. All the galaxies make up the universe. No one knows where the universe begins or ends. We don't know how big the universe is. We don't know when it began or when it will end. We don't know if it did ever begin or if it will ever end. We don't know if it's getting bigger or smaller. We don't know if it has a shape. We don't know where the earth is in the universe. We don't know why the universe is here at all.'

'Oh no,' said the plastic skeleton. 'I can't stand this stuff. He always brings it round to that. I'd rather talk to the wall than listen to this rubbish bag.'

Frank had listened to what the space suit had said and though he didn't think he had understood everything it had said, he knew that suddenly he felt very, very small.

The plastic skeleton looked down at Frank. 'Now come on, boy, don't stand there like that.'

'Where's my mum?' said Frank.

'Where's the real wild man of Ashton Forest?' said the plastic skeleton.

'I don't know,' said Frank.

'Watch this,' said the plastic skeleton. 'Mission

Control to Space Suit One. Join us in the wild man search. Roger.'

'Space Suit to Mission Control. You're looking good. No, I mean, I'm looking good. Who cares? *We're* looking good, huh? Sure love to come on wild man search. Great. Roger.'

'He'll help us find your mum as well, if you ask him.'

So Frank said, 'Will you help us find – '

'No not like that,' said the plastic skeleton. 'Give him orders. Mission Control, and all that.'

So Frank said, 'Mission Control to Space Suit One. Help find my mum as well.'

'Space Suit One to Mission Control. It's a great little world you've got out there. Let's go, let's go. We'll find mum. Terrific! I like it. Roger.'

'See,' said the plastic skeleton.

So without any more hanging around, Frank, the plastic skeleton of the wild man of Ashton Forest and the space suit walked off across the shiny museum floor.

'I just hope Mrs Longstone doesn't see us,' said the plastic skeleton to Frank.

'I just hope the stone men don't come after us again,' said Frank.

'That's one small step for a man, one giant leap for bubble gum,' said the space suit.

'Oh shuttup,' said the plastic skeleton of the wild man of Ashton Forest.

Chapter Five

'THIS WAY, GUYS,' said the space suit, 'you're look-ing good. Channel zero plus. You ain't seen nothing yet.' The space suit was leading Frank and the plas-tic skeleton towards the bottom of the stairs. These stairs were great wide steps leading to the upstairs gal-leries, and all the way up the stairs were various stuffed animals. On the landing halfway up, was the tiger that Frank had dreamed about.

'Come on, boy,' said the plastic skeleton, 'you never know, this space suit might have a programme inside it to find your mum.'

But Frank hung back. He trusted his feelings and his feelings were telling him, 'Don't go up those stairs past that tiger.'

'Come on, boy,' said the plastic skeleton, 'we might even find those peanuts you were thinking about.'

'I wasn't thinking about peanuts,' said Frank.

'Yes you were,' said the plastic skeleton, 'but don't worry about it. You have to think about something, don't you? Some people think about macaroni cheese.'

'I sometimes think about macaroni cheese,' said Frank.

'Do you?' said the plastic skeleton. 'You should see a doctor. That's very very worrying. You could become very very ill thinking about macaroni cheese.'

'Could I?' said Frank.

'That's how I got ill,' said the plastic skeleton, 'thinking about macaroni cheese.'

'But you've never been alive,' said Frank, 'how could you have got ill?'

'I know what you're thinking,' said the plastic skeleton, not answering Frank's question, 'you're thinking that if you go on talking to me we won't have to go up the stairs past the tiger you're scared of.'

'Yes' said Frank in that small voice.

'Well, listen,' said the plastic skeleton, 'I don't think you're the only one who's scared. Look at Space Suit over there.'

Space Suit was standing very still with one foot on the bottom step.

'It looks like an exhibit in a museum,' said the plastic skeleton.

'It *is* an exhibit in a museum, isn't it?' said Frank.

'Well,' said the plastic skeleton, 'it's not surprising that it looks like one then, is it, boy?'

The tiger moved.

'Oh no,' thought Frank. 'This is horrible.'

'It moved,' said Frank.

'I know she did,' said the plastic skeleton.

'I'm scared,' said Frank.

'I know you are,' said the plastic skeleton.

'It's coming downstairs,' said Frank.

'I know she is,' said the plastic skeleton.

'Can't Space Suit do something?'

'No,' said the plastic skeleton.

Just then, the tiger seemed to have noticed Space Suit. It took a step backwards, crouched down and tried to hide itself.

'Right, come on,' said the plastic skeleton. 'Mission Control to Space Suit One. Keep going, Roger.'

And Space Suit said, 'Hi, hi, guys, easy as she goes. Wow. We're really cooking!'

So now, all three of them walked up the stairs towards the tiger, Frank hiding behind the other two. Step by step they went. Frank was amazed to see the plastic skeleton walk towards the tiger and bend down to talk to it. The tiger crouched in a huddle, so Frank stepped a bit nearer so he could hear what the plastic skeleton was saying:

'. . . It's all right, Tiger. He won't harm you. It's only Space Suit. There's no one inside it. Don't worry. Don't panic. It's all right.'

And all the while, Tiger was moaning and saying, 'No, no, no. I don't want to be killed again. No, no.'

The plastic skeleton went on being kind, 'It's all right, Tiger. He won't harm you. He hasn't got a gun. He can't harm you.'

Frank remembered the rockets. He wasn't so sure. But in the end Tiger got up.

'Now, come on,' said the plastic skeleton, 'you

come and say hallo to Space Suit.'

So, very, very slowly Tiger loped towards Space Suit. 'Hallo,' said Tiger.

'Hi,' said Space Suit, 'This is great. It's a great day. Terrific! Hi. Nice day. Really nice.'

Tiger looked at Space Suit.

'Now come and say hallo to Frank,' said the plastic skeleton.

Tiger loped towards Frank. 'Hallo.'

Frank just stared. He was terrified.

'No need to be scared of me,' said Tiger, 'I'm dead. I died in India years ago. I used to be dangerous. I used to be wild. I used to be a great powerful beast that could move through long grass with such speed, all people could see of me was a golden streak of light.'

'What happened to you?' said Frank, 'What did you die of?'

Tiger dropped her head and looked sad. 'I was killed.'

'OK guys, let's move it. OK? Let's move it. That's one small step for a man one giant leap for Tarzan and The Giant Crab.'

'Oh shuttup,' said the plastic skeleton. 'You must listen to this,' it said to Frank. 'Go on, Tiger.'

'I thought I was big and strong enough never to be trapped or killed by such a weak creature as a man. I knew I had such power in my body.'

'It happened like this. I had killed a deer for my three cubs to eat and we sat by the side of a river feeding, when suddenly I heard distant noises. It was the sound of trees and bushes breaking, men's voices shouting, the thud of elephants' feet. I could smell the men and their food and their drink and I could smell hundreds of elephants. At first, I thought maybe it was a fire and people were running away, but then suddenly, I realized they weren't running away from anything. They were hunting me. The deer I had caught was bait, that they had put out for me. I had been tricked. At first I could only hear the noise from one side and I thought I could escape with my three cubs, so I stayed where I was, where we were safe, with food. I wasn't afraid. I knew I was strong. I knew I was fast. I knew I was powerful. But the noise got louder and the smells got stronger. And then, I realized that the elephants were not just on one side. They were all round me. There was a ring right round me of over a hundred elephants. On top of each elephant sat an Indian man and every so often there was an Englishman with a gun. These men shouted at the Indians, telling them to move on, near-er and nearer to me. I crouched down low with my cubs thinking we wouldn't be seen, but the great crashing and smashing of the bushes and trees went on; birds flew up into the sky, rats rushed out of the way. I found myself thinking, why would the ele-phants harm me? I never harm elephants. But these elephants were the servants of men and each man could control an elephant with a sharp stick. Then as one part of the circle came nearer, I could see that on one of the elephants sat an Englishman who everyone thought was very important. Servants were fanning him and bringing him drinks. He was King George the Fifth. Hundreds of men and animals and guns had been got together so that King George the Fifth could kill me. I felt a terrible panic grip me. I knew I was about to lose my cubs. The ones I had spent so much care and strength on, hiding them, hunting for them, nursing them. I looked at them and straight-away, I knew what to do: urge them to run at the ring of elephants. Perhaps to break through between two elephants in the ring, perhaps the men with guns wouldn't shoot at them. So I forced my three cubs for-wards, and they broke out of our hiding place and into the open. Immediately, I heard the rifles fire. A crack louder than the shouting and the trampling. But then I saw one, then two cubs reach the ring of elephants. Two of them moved apart and let my cubs through. So, it had been a mistake. The men hadn't meant to fire at my cubs. They had thought one or perhaps both of them were me, streaking out of the bushes. But where was my third cub? I couldn't see her anywhere. And then, as I moved myself, I saw her stretched out on her side, blood dripping from her neck. Fear and hate and sadness came to me all at the same time. I felt a wave of force pass into my back and down my legs and I found myself leaping for-wards, roaring from the bottom of my throat. I plun-ged through the bushes and long grass. I could see the row of elephants ahead I had to break through. I had to be free. I had to reach my two cubs. But just as I came leaping through, I saw a long narrow metal rifle pointing at me from King George the Fifth's chair. There was a flash of fire, a crack that broke my ears and a tearing, burning pain in my chest, a terrible smell of metal and smoke and blood. All the strength of my front legs and chest rushed from me, but the

power in my back legs pushed me on. I rolled for-
wards and fell. A hard numb feeling moved through
me. My eyes blurred over. I saw the men waving in
the air. I saw nothing. I heard nothing. I felt nothing.
I was dead.'

Frank didn't know if he felt sad or angry. He just
looked at Tiger and wanted to go up to her and touch
her or hug her or something. Instead he just said in
that small voice, 'How did you get here?'

'I'm a present. A present from King George the
Fifth. They took out my bones, they stuffed me with
some hairy stuff and here I am at the top of the stairs
with my mouth open to make me look fierce and
angry. It's supposed to make you think how brave the
king was to have shot such a dangerous beast as me.
Him and his hundreds of elephants and men and
guns shot thirty-nine tigers that month, in the year
1911. I hear there are not many of us left out there
now.'

'Well, wow,' said Space Suit, 'that's really something. That's one small step for a man, one giant leap
for popcorn.'

'Oh do shuttup,' said the plastic skeleton. 'I'm sorry,' it said to Tiger, 'but he has no idea what's going
on.'

'That's all right,' said Tiger, 'neither did King
George the Fifth.'

'Did he used to say all that, 'one-small-step-for-
man' stuff?' said Frank.

'No,' said Tiger, 'he kept firing his gun and saying, "Have I bagged it?" "Oh what a fine bag." "That's a jolly good bag for an afternoon." You'd've thought he was talking about handbags or something.'

'What *was* he talking about?' said Frank.

'Us. Dead tigers. He had got us. Bagged us. Do you understand?'

'Yes,' said Frank, but now all he could think of was that the King of England thought the tiger was a handbag. Frank didn't know what to say, so he said, 'We're looking for my mum.'

But the moment he said it, he realized it was a silly thing to say to Tiger. She immediately thought of her dead cub and the two who had got through the ring of elephants. The ones she had never seen again.

The plastic skeleton saw her looking sad, so *he* said, '*And* we're looking for the real wild man of Ashton Forest.'

'Yippeeee,' said Space Suit.

'Shuttup,' said the plastic skeleton.

'Do you want to come?' said Frank.

'No,' said Tiger. 'Give me a shout if you want some help. I don't like the look of your astronaut friend there. He looks like he might do something crazy any moment.'

'Oh no,' said the plastic skeleton, 'he's on a safe programme at the moment.'

'Oh yes,' said Tiger, 'if that's the safe one, what's the unsafe one like?'

'Oh you know,' said the plastic skeleton, 'firing rockets.'

'Oh yes, I understand,' said Tiger. 'I understand that very well.'

'What do you understand?' said Frank.

'Don't bother her any more, boy,' said the plastic skeleton, 'we must hurry up now or it'll be time for me to get back in my case.'

'Do we have lift-off?' said Space Suit.

'We do,' said the plastic skeleton.

'Goodbye, Tiger,' said Frank.

'So long, sweetie face!' said Space Suit.

'What idiot thought it was a good idea to bring this fathead along?' said the plastic skeleton.

'*You're* the idiot that thought it was a good idea to bring that fathead along,' said Frank.

'Oh,' said the plastic skeleton, and on they went up the stairs.

Chapter Six

A BIT FURTHER up the stairs the plastic skeleton said, 'We could talk to the witch.'

'Terrific,' said Space Suit.

'Where is she?' said Frank.

'Where⁄she⁄isn't,' said the plastic skeleton.

'Where is Where⁄she⁄isn't?' said Frank.

'There,' said the plastic skeleton and he pointed at a kind of chair with a metal cage round it. 'That's Where⁄she⁄isn't,' said the plastic skeleton.

'We do not see it, we do NOT see it,' said Space Suit. 'That's one small step for a man, one giant leap for "The Invisible Man".'

'I can't see her either,' said Frank. 'Can she help us?'

'I don't think so,' said the plastic skeleton, 'because she's not there.'

'But you said we could talk to the witch,' said Frank.

'Of course I did,' said the plastic skeleton, 'but I didn't say she'd talk to *us*.'

'We might as well talk to the wall,' said Frank.

'Oh no,' said the plastic skeleton, 'talking to the wall is talking to no one. We can talk to someone who isn't there. That's much more interesting.'

'Was she ever there?' said Frank.

'Ask her,' said the plastic skeleton.

Frank went up to the empty chair, 'Were you ever there?' said Frank to the empty space in the cage.

There was no answer.

'But you haven't said who she is. She doesn't know you're talking to her,' said the plastic skeleton.

'Excuse me, hallo, witch,' said Frank.

There was no answer again.

'Receiving you, great. Terrific,' said Space Suit.

'What's he receiving?' said Frank.

'I don't know,' said the plastic skeleton, 'but he'll receive a kick up the pants if he doesn't keep quiet.'

'She hasn't answered,' said Frank.

'Why not?' said the plastic skeleton.

'I was going to ask *you* that,' said Frank.

'I asked *you* though,' said the plastic skeleton.

'Why hasn't she answered?' said Frank to himself.

'Why hasn't she answered? I've got it . . . because someone else is there who isn't a witch.'

'Now you're talking,' said Space Suit.

'I wasn't talking,' said Frank. 'I was thinking.'

'Hallo,' he tried again, 'are you someone else who isn't there?'

'Hallo,' said a woman's voice, 'can you help me find my mum?'

'I was going to say that,' said Frank

'I said it first,' said the woman's voice.

'I can't even find *you*,' said Frank, 'so how am I going to find your mum?'

'I'm not here. That's where I am,' said the woman's voice.

'Why aren't you here?' said Frank.

'Because I am who I am,' said the woman's voice.

'Can we go now,' said Frank, 'I'm going mad.'

'Me too,' said the woman's voice.

'Me too, guys,' said Space Suit.

'Look,' said Frank, getting cross, 'if you're not who you are, and you're not where you are and you're going mad, what are you doing here? I mean what are you doing *not* here?'

'I'm locked in,' said the woman's voice.

Frank looked into the cage very hard, and at the chair. It explained something underneath. It said they used to lock women into this chair and it was put up and down into a river. There was a picture.

'You're reading it, aren't you?' said the woman's voice.

'Yes,' said Frank.

'Reading you loud and clear,' said Space Suit.

'Switch yourself off, will you?' said the plastic skeleton.

Suddenly the picture Frank was looking at came to life, like a film. The woman in the chair was screaming terribly. Frank felt the skin on the back of his neck hurt just hearing this terrible scream. Then suddenly, the woman, the cage and the chair went plunging down into the river, and the woman was held under the water inside the cage. There was a crowd of people on the river bank and they were shouting, 'Witch, witch, witch.' Others were shouting, 'Hold her down, keep her in there.' Then up she came again and water was streaming from the chair and the woman's clothes and hair. Once more the terrible screaming came from the woman, but she was gasping and choking. She called out, 'Mother, save me.'

And then Frank saw an old woman on the river bank struggling to reach the people pushing the see-saw up and down, but the people wouldn't let her get near, and pushed her away easily.

Frank heard people yelling again. 'She came to my house begging for corn. When I gave her none, my chickens choked to death on the corn I gave them,' said one.

'She came to my house begging for milk. When I gave her none, my cow's milk came out as blood,' said another.

'She came to my house begging for bread. When I gave her none, my child fell on the floor and foamed at the mouth,' said another.

'Drown her, drown her, drown her,' they screamed.

Down she went again and once more up. The screaming had stopped and the woman sat there, limp and soft, the water still streaming from her chair, her dress, and her hair. Then the picture froze.

'I was a beggar,' said the woman's voice, 'that's all, and they didn't want to give me anything. I couldn't feed myself.'

'So,' said the plastic skeleton. 'You are the witch who isn't there, aren't you? Why didn't you answer before, eh?'

There was silence.

'Where's she gone?' said Frank.

'There's one helluva big nowhere out there, kid,' said Space Suit.

'She's gone to where she isn't,' said the plastic skeleton.

'You've frightened her off,' said Frank.

'She's not real anyway,' said the plastic skeleton.

'Neither are you,' said Frank.

'I'm real er than her. At least I'm a copy of the real wild man. She isn't even who she is. She isn't even where she is. I know who I am, boy, and don't forget it, all right?'

'Information received OK OK OK, great thing, guys,' said Space Suit.

'Give him a doughnut,' said the plastic skeleton.

'I hope you find *your* mum,' said Frank to the cage, and he thought he heard one more tiny faraway scream.

Chapter Seven

WHEN THEY GOT to the top of the stairs, Space Suit said, 'Hey, hold it there, guys, This is really high up, you know. This is one small step for a man, one giant leap for an air disaster.'

'What's he going on about?' said the plastic skeleton.

'I don't think he likes heights.'

'Hey wow. Scare-eeee. It's one helluva way up and one helluva way down. I can't take this, Buster.'

'Oh come along, I thought you had been twenty miles up in the air, been weightless and walked outside a space ship,' said the plastic skeleton.

There was silence.

'Well, haven't you?' said the plastic skeleton.

Silence.

'Mission Control to Space Suit One: Have you ever been weightless? Have you ever been up in a space ship? Have you ever walked outside?'

'Space Suit to Mission Control: No, no, no.'

'Mission Control to Space Suit One: But it says on your label you were the space suit worn by John McKinley on Space Shuttle Flight ND650.'

'Space Suit One to Mission Control: I was nearly

the space suit worn by John McKinley.'

The plastic skeleton looked at Frank. Frank look⁄ed at the plastic skeleton. Frank said, 'I don't think a space suit that's afraid of heights is going to help me find my mum.'

The plastic skeleton said, 'I don't think a space suit that's afraid of heights is going to help us do any⁄thing.'

Frank said, 'I wonder how much it cost.'

The plastic skeleton said, 'Maybe we could sell it and buy some of those doughnuts you keep going on about.'

'I hate doughnuts,' said Frank.

'Then why do you keep going on about them?' said the plastic skeleton. 'That's your problem, boy, if you could just relax a bit about doughnuts, you wouldn't keep going on about them. Relax, boy, relax.'

'OK,' said Frank, hoping that if he agreed with the plastic skeleton it would stop him going on about these darned doughnuts.

'Right, let's go,' said the plastic skeleton, 'We'll leave Space Suit here.'

'That's one small step for a man, one giant leap for a –'

'We're going to the Bartlett Gallery now.' So Frank and the plastic skeleton walked into the part of the museum called the Bartlett Gallery.

The moment they walked through the door, there was a great chorus of voices: 'Oh no, look who's

come in here now.'

All sorts of posh voices started calling out things:
'Oh, it's that awful skeleton fellow.' 'Who's the boy?'
'I think it's the ghastly cleaner woman's son. Oh how
frightful.'

Frank looked round to see who could be talking
like that, but all he could see were old dolls and puppets and old children's toys.

'Oh my dear,' said a little brown toy pig, 'look at
him now. The awful little brat is looking at us. It makes
me feel dirty just to think of him looking at me.'

The plastic skeleton could see Frank was getting
upset again.

'Hallo snobs,' said the plastic skeleton, in a loud
mocking voice.

'Oh dear, he's talking to us now,' said a batteredup tin soldier, 'Who does he think he is, that skeleton
fellow?'

'Life's bad enough sitting in this place without louts
like him coming and talking to us,' said Mr Punch.

'How are you feeling today, you lot?' said the plastic skeleton.

'Why are you talking to them?' said Frank. 'They don't want to talk to you.'

'Oh don't take any notice of the way they talk. That's all put on,' said the plastic skeleton.

'Why do they do it then?'

'I'll tell you. Most of these dolls and toys and Punch and Judys were once toys. Children played with them. Then they were collected.'

'We were collected, we were collected, and so we were,' called out Judy's dog, Toby.

'Collected what?' said Frank.

Hoots of laughter from the toys. 'Wha wha wha whaaa.'

'No,' said the plastic skeleton, 'Jeremiah Bartlett collected them.'

'Why?' said Frank.

'Why?' said the tatty little tin soldier mockingly, 'Why? Oh, the dear boy is so ignorant. Because we're beautiful, you fool.'

'And perfect little treasures,' said the Punch-and-Judy crocodile.

'We are worth hundreds and hundreds of pounds, young man,' said Judy.

'Why?' said Frank.

'Why? Why?' said the tin soldier. 'There he goes again. Because we were collected. We are simply adorable little things.'

And everyone cheered and laughed.

'We are all adorable little things.'

'But you're just Punch and Judy,' said Frank. 'Punch doesn't talk like you, he says: "That's the way to do it" in a squeaky voice. And he's common, not posh like you.'

'Oh stop him, someone. The frightful little cleaner boy is talking absolute bilge. I am not any old Mr Punch, you fool, I am The Bartlett Punch.'

Frank liked it that he annoyed this horrible Mr Punch. So he said, 'That's the way to do it,' again.

Mr Punch hated him for it and turned away. 'Talk to him, Judy. I can't bear to look at him.'

'All this lot were collected by a rich old man called Bartlett,' said the plastic skeleton, 'and when he died, they sold off his big country house and the museum got all of them.'

'Oh for goodness sake, wild man, don't remind us,' said the pig. 'There we were in this beautiful place, Bartlett Manor, with decent people coming to see us and suddenly we were put on show here in the . . . City Museum . . . (He made "City Museum" sound as if it was a dung heap) . . . for people like that awful cleaner boy to come and stare at us. And schoolchildren. It's unbearable.'

'But you're just a little pig,' said Frank.

'Oh get him out of here,' said the pig. 'I can't stand his way of talking.'

'I have heard the Duke of Rochester wanted to

buy me, you know,' said Toby the dog.

'That's the way to do it,' said Frank really horribly and loudly.

'I know how to get rid of him,' said one of the dolls. 'Oh come on, Annabelle, say it.'

'I know where his mother is,' said Annabelle.

'Oh you're wonderful, Annabelle,' said the crocodile, 'tease him, tease him.'

So Annabelle the doll piped up again and spoke to Frank directly. 'I know where your mother is.'

'Where?' said Frank.

'Oh, now look at him, the little lout has changed his tune now,' said Mr Punch.

'Make him say please,' said the pig.

'Please, madam, you mean,' said Mr Punch.

The plastic skeleton turned to Frank: 'She probably knows. You may have to ask her, boy.'

'Where's my mum?' said Frank.

Annabelle wouldn't answer.

'Say, "please madam",' said the pig.

'Where's my mum, please madam?'

And all the toys burst out laughing and clapping. 'You've made the lout say it, you've made the lout say it. That'll teach the brat. Manners boy, eh what?'

'Well?' said Frank.

'Well, what?' said the pig.

'Well, madam,' said Frank looking at the doll.

'Your mother has been caught by Mr Bryman and she is working for him now.'

Frank looked at the plastic skeleton.

The plastic skeleton looked the other way.

'What does that mean?' said Frank.

'I'm afraid it's rather bad news,' said the plastic skeleton.

Frank was worried. 'Where is she? What's going on? Who's Mr Bryman?'

'Ha ha ha, that's worried him. He won't come round here with his rude talk again, the little brat,' said the pig.

This made Frank angry. Really wild, in fact. Scarcely caring what he was doing, he pulled open one of the cases of the Bartlett Collection. He grab-bed Mr Punch and the Punch-and-Judy hangman and started jigging them up and down.

He made Mr Punch say, 'That's the way to do it.'

Then he made the hangman say, 'I'll hang you, Mr Punch, I'll hang you, Mr Punch.'

'Oh no you won't,' said Frank, shaking Punch.

'Oh yes I will,' said Frank, shaking the hangman.

Punch and the hangman were livid. 'Put us down, you lout. Let go, you hooligan. We're not for playing with. We're not puppets. We're beautiful things.'

But Frank went on. 'Here's the rope, Mr Punch, and I'm going to hang you till you're dead,' said Frank, shaking the hangman.

'No, no, no, don't do it Mr Hangman,' said Frank, shaking Punch.

'Yes, yes, yes,' said Frank, shaking the hangman.

Frank got the rope ready. 'Put me down, put me down,' said Punch.

'Where's my mum?' said Frank.

'With Mr Bryman,' said Punch.

'Where's Mr Bryman?' said Frank and he shook the two puppets together till their heads cracked together.

'How dare you, how dare you, we're worth thousands of pounds. We're not for handling. You've cracked us. You've cracked my beautiful head.'

'Where's Mr Bryman?' said Frank.

'He's in the glass house. Put me down. Put me down.'

The plastic skeleton was enjoying all this a lot. He had never dared do it himself though he hated the Bartlett Collection.

'Come on, boy, I know the way. We'd better hurry. Your mum could be in trouble.'

'What do you mean? My "mum could be in trouble"?' said Frank.

'I mean your mum could be in trouble,' said the plastic skeleton.

'Oh,' said Frank, 'thanks for telling me.'

'That's all right, boy,' said the plastic skeleton, 'I'll always explain something you don't understand. Just ask me. Now put those two little chaps back in their case and let's go.'

'Coming,' said Frank.

And off they went to the glass house.

Chapter Eight

'HAVE YOU GOT the doughnuts with you?' said the plastic skeleton.

'No,' said Frank.

'You had the bag, didn't you, boy?' said the plastic skeleton.

'I didn't have a bag,' said Frank.

'Think, boy.'

'I am,' said Frank.

'You must try,' said the plastic skeleton.

'Try what?' said Frank.

'Try harder,' said the plastic skeleton.

'OK,' said Frank, though he had no idea what he was trying harder to do.

By now, they had arrived in The Science Box, on the way to the glass house.

Elvis Presley was there to meet them . . . 'Hallo,' he said. 'Nice to see you. We're going to have a lovely time. It's going to be really super. So come along. Join in. Make it a lovely day for all the family. I ain't nothing but a houndog.'

Frank stared at him. He thought Elvis was American. But this Elvis was talking in a very polite English voice even when he said, 'I ain't nothing but a houndog'.

Then, just as he was trying to work this out, Marilyn Monroe popped her head round the edge of a pillar. She spoke the same way. 'Halloooo. Come on in. It's going to be really super. You're going to find out all about how things work.'

'And how things don't work,' said Elvis.

'You're in the brand new Science Box, you know. Lots of fun for all the family,' said Elvis.

'This is a fly,' said Marilyn Monroe. And a great big fly, about as big as a piano, flew down from the ceiling.

'Hi there,' said the giant fly in a very slow deep bored voice. 'I'm a fly.'

'You know,' said Elvis, getting excited, 'flies have hairs all over them. Isn't that interesting?'

'Yeah,' said the giant fly in his slow bored voice, 'I've got really interesting hairs.'

'When he eats,' said Marilyn, 'he puts a little tube down onto the food. Out comes some stuff like the spit in your mouth, and then – '

'Wait for it,' said Elvis, 'this is really interesting –'

'– he draws it up the tube.'

'Yeah,' said the giant fly, 'Really interesting. First I spit. Then I suck. Cor.'

'What do you think, Henry?' said Elvis to Frank.

'My name's Frank,' said Frank.

'You think it's jolly interesting, that's what you think,' said Marilyn, 'don't you, Henry?'

'Er . . . I don't know,' said Frank.

'Got any biscuits?' said the giant fly.

'Keep your mouth shut, Fly,' said Elvis, out the corner of his mouth,

'I haven't got a mouth,' said the giant fly, 'I've got a proboscis.'

'Then keep your proboscis shut,' said Elvis.

'Now, Henry, do you want to see the embryo? Yes you do want to see the embryo,' said Marilyn.

'I don't know what an embryo is,' said Frank.

'It's a baby when it's still inside it's mummy's tummy. You were once an embryo, Henry.'

'I don't want to see the embryo,' said Frank. 'I want to see my mum.'

'That's just what Embryo thinks,' said Elvis, Cooooo-eeeee, Embee!'

And a big plastic embryo waddled out of a dark corner.

'He's got fingernails, Henry,' said Elvis in a wild excited voice.

'My name's Frank,' said Frank.

'He's got fingernails. Wooopeee. I ain't nothing but a houndog.'

'He's got fingernails,' said Marilyn, 'isn't that interesting?'

'I don't know,' said Frank. 'How do we get to the glass house. I'm a bit worried about my mum.'

'You can't go yet, Henry,' said Elvis, 'This is fun for all the family.' He grabbed hold of Frank's arm. Rather hard.

'I haven't told you about Embryo's toenails, yet,' said Marilyn, and she grabbed Frank's other arm. 'Are you having a good time, Henry?'

'No,' said Frank. 'Let go.'

'No, you're here to have a good time,' said Elvis.

'But I'm not having a good time,' said Frank.

'Listen here,' said Elvis, 'we know the answers to all the questions in the world.'

'Where's my mum?' said Frank.

'We know the answers to all the questions in the world except that one,' Marilyn Monroe said.

'We know everything,' said Elvis, 'and you'd better believe it, sonny.'

'Why are you twisting my arm?' said Frank.

'That's not a real question,' Marilyn said, 'so we don't have to answer it.'

'What is it, then, if it's not a real question?' said Frank.

'That's not a real question either. We're not answering it.'

'That's three questions you haven't answered,' said Frank.

'Listen,' said Elvis, 'never mind that. Just remember we know the answers to all the questions in the world. Believe it. OK? Believe it.'

'Tell them to let go of me,' Frank said to the plastic skeleton.

I can't' said the plastic skeleton. 'No one takes any notice of me up here. I'm part of the Old Museum. This is the New Museum.'

'Let go,' said Frank.

'No,' said Elvis, 'you've got to stay here and listen to us.'

So Frank twisted one way and then the other. He broke his arm loose from Elvis but Marilyn still had hold of him.

'Help me,' said Frank to the plastic skeleton.

'I can't,' said the plastic skeleton, 'I'm from downstairs.'

'Come and have some more fun, Henry,' said

Marilyn.

'No,' said Frank, and bit her arm. She let go. Frank got free and ran.

The plastic skeleton joined him.

They just heard the giant fly talking as they were going.

'Well,' it was saying in that slow bored voice, 'that didn't look like they thought you two were a bundle of laughs.'

'I'll tie your proboscis up if you don't keep quiet,' said Elvis.

'Oh yes,' said the giant fly, 'try explaining a proboscis with a knot in it, as part of your fun for All the Family.'

Frank heard Elvis trying to tie up the giant fly's proboscis as they hurried round the corner into the glass house.

Chapter Nine

'WE MUST HURRY,' said the plastic skeleton. 'We haven't got much time. I'll have to get back in my glass case soon. And you must be starving hungry. Probably there aren't any doughnuts left by now.'

'Where *are* the doughnuts?' said Frank.

'I don't know,' said the plastic skeleton.

'Well, then, it doesn't matter if there *are* doughnuts or if there *aren't* doughnuts,' said Frank, 'we still can't have any.'

'Don't get sulky with me, boy,' said the plastic skeleton.

'*I'm* thinking about doughnuts,' said a slow tired bored voice behind them.

They looked round. It was the giant fly.

'Aren't you supposed to be in The Science Box?' said the plastic skeleton.

'I escaped,' said the giant fly. 'I'm giving up Fun For All The Family.'

'What are you going to do now, then?' said Frank.

'I'd like to run a sports shop. You know, selling sweatshirts and trainers and things.'

'What are you going to call your shop?' said Frank

'The Great Big Fly,' said the giant fly.

'But that's got nothing to do with sweatshirts and trainers,' said Frank. 'I mean, you're not going to sell great big flies there, are you?'

'So?', said the giant fly, 'at the Old Red Lion Pub, they don't sell old red lions, do they?'

'Look,' said the plastic skeleton, 'we're in a hurry. We've got to find the real skeleton of the wild man of Ashton Forest.'

'And my mum,' said Frank.

'And my sports shop,' said the giant fly.

'And my mum's with Mr Bryman,' said Frank, 'and he's in the glass house.'

'So are we,' said the giant fly.

It was right. They had arrived in the glass house.

The glass house was a small hall with a glass roof in it. On one side stood a statue of a man with a military hat on. Underneath it said 'General Fawcett.' Frank glanced at it. He remembered the name from the stone men and it made him scared to think of it. He quickly looked away from the statue. On the other side was a white stone statue of a large plump man. Underneath his feet was a plaque that said,

'Joseph Bryman. This museum was founded with the kind financial assistance of Joseph Bryman. To him we owe much thanks. Herbert and Sybil Longstone.'

'What's "financial assistance"?' said Frank.

'Money,' said the giant fly. 'Some people don't like to call money, "money", so they call it other things.'

62

'Like doughnuts,' said the plastic skeleton.

'Some people would write,' said the plastic skeleton, 'This museum was founded with the kind doughnuts of Joseph Bryman.' Frank giggled. Then he remembered that this Bryman was something to do with his mother. 'What does he do?' he said.

'He had lots of doughnuts,' said the plastic skeleton.

'Money,' said the giant fly.

'He wanted people to like him so he gave a load of doughnuts to Mr and Mrs Longstone to start the museum, a hundred years ago. He said they could have his doughnuts so long as he could have a statue of himself in the museum. So here it is.'

'The Longstones,' said Frank. 'I've heard of them. Mrs Longstone. I've seen her. She told the stone men off.'

'It's not only the stone men she tells off. You ought to hear her telling Mr Longstone off.'

Frank looked back at Joseph Bryman. 'Where did he get all his money from?' he said.

'Pickled onions,' said the giant fly.

The moment the giant fly said that, the plastic skeleton started spinning round, jumping up and down and getting very excited.

'What's the matter?' said Frank.

'Not doughnuts – pickled onions. I'm sorry, boy. I'm really sorry. All this time I've been talking about doughnuts. I meant pickled onions.'

'Did you?' said Frank. 'Well I wasn't even think-ing about pickled onions, either.'

'He hasn't got a brain,' said the giant fly, 'So he does very well. But every now and then he makes a mistake.'

'It's not my fault I haven't got a brain,' said the plastic skeleton. 'I'm all plastic.'

'Me too,' said the giant fly, 'but they gave me a plastic brain.'

'OK. They forgot to give me one. Don't go on about it,' said the plastic skeleton. 'Doughnuts – pickled onions. Anyone could think a pickled onion was a doughnut, couldn't they?'

Frank and the giant fly looked at each other.

'Actually er . . . no,' said the giant fly, 'I can't think of anyone who would think a pickled onion was a doughnut.'

'But plenty of people could think money was doughnuts or pickled onions, couldn't they?' said the plastic skeleton. 'That's what I'm trying to say. It's all the same stuff.'

'Where's my mum?' said Frank, 'I don't know what you're talking about again.'

'She's probably in Joseph Bryman's pickled onion factory,' said the giant fly, 'making Bryman's pickled onions, Bryman's pickled cabbage, Bryman's piccalil-li or Bryman's military pickle.

'I want to go there,' said Frank.

'Oh do you?' said the giant fly. 'You'll have to do

one or two things first. We'll all stand in front of the statue and have a look at Joseph Bryman.'

So the giant fly, the plastic skeleton and Frank looked up at Joseph Bryman. He had furry bits down the side of his face, a waistcoat and big laced up shoes. It said on the statue that he died in 1895.

'Right, say after me,' said the giant fly, 'Joseph Bryman, you are a good and kind man.'

Frank said it.

'For many years you have been good and kind enough to give work to the people of this city.'

Frank said it.

'You have been good and kind enough to make pickles, and good and kind enough to give money to this museum,' the giant fly went on in his bored voice. 'The people of this city will remember you forever and just in case we don't, we come and look at this lovely statue of you.'

Frank said all this too.

'Now watch,' said the giant fly. 'He loves all that so much, he wakes up.'

And sure enough, the statue began to move. The eyes sparkled and there was Joseph Bryman. 'Aha,' said the statue in a loud deep voice. 'At last someone who appreciates me. Someone who admires me, sees me for who I am. A kind and good man.'

The giant fly interrupted, 'No you're not. You're very horrible and very boring.'

Frank was shocked. 'But you just told me to say

that he was good and kind.'

'That was to wake him up, you fool. He can't do anything about it now.'

Frank looked up at him and thought he looked very big and very strong.

'Don't worry,' said the plastic skeleton, 'He can't get off there. He's up there on show forever. That's the way he wanted it to be.'

'Aha, where was I?' said Bryman.

'It doesn't matter,' said the giant fly, 'we don't want to listen.'

'Where's the boy's mum?' said the plastic skeleton.

'I have given her work,' said Mr Bryman.

'Oh no, she is in the pickle factory,' said the plastic skeleton.

'How do we get there?' said Frank. He was worried. Maybe his mum was being made into pickles.

'I can't see it here,' said Frank

'Of course not,' said the giant fly. 'No one who comes here is supposed to know about Bryman's pickles factory.'

'Don't you dare show people round my factory,' said Bryman.

The giant fly stepped up to the statue and said, 'Great man, great statue,' and Joseph Bryman turned back to being a statue.

'Why did you do that?' said Frank, 'I want to know where the factory is.'

'They pulled it down years ago. It's disappeared

66

and forgotten about.'

'Well, if they pulled it down, how come my mum's in there?'

'The factory is in his heart,' said the giant fly.

'I want to see it,' said Frank.

'All right,' said the giant fly, 'but I warn you. What you see might upset you.'

'Maybe they *are* turning her into pickles,' said Frank to himself.

The giant fly climbed up the statue, opened Bryman's waistcoat and then opened a little door in his chest.

'Come and look in here,' said the giant fly.

Frank stood up on tip toe and peeped in through the door in Joseph Bryman's chest. In there, it was like a moving model. It was a long, low, dark room with lamps burning. Rows of women stood at benches. Some were chopping vegetables, some were pputting them in jars, some were mixing, some were sticking labels saying JOSEPH BRYMAN onto the jars, some were pouring things into the jars.

The place was completely quiet. A man with a tall hat walked up and down the rows of women, stopping every now and then to tap one on the shoulder with his stick. Frank could smell the air. It was vinegary and very cold.

Some of the women had no shoes on. Some were shivering. 'Are they chopping mum up?' thought Frank.

Then suddenly, on one end of a row, he saw someone who looked like his mum. She had her hands in a bowl, but her arms were yellow up to above her elbows. She was making piccalilli – a mustard pick⁄le. The rest of her arms and her face had big white rings on as if her skin was just about to peel off.

'Mum,' shouted Frank, 'MUM!'

'She can't hear you,' said the giant fly, 'and anyway she's not allowed to talk while she's working.'

'Why not?' said Frank.

'In case she stops working,' said the giant fly.

'But she could work *and* talk couldn't she?' said Frank.

'Mr Bryman says she can't,' said the giant fly.

'It's not my mum then. She wouldn't stand for that.'

He watched the woman. Maybe it *was* Mum. 'She looks very tired,' he said. 'She looks like she's going to drop down and fall over at any moment. They all do.'

'They work there from seven o'clock in the morn⁄ing until nine o'clock at night. And they don't eat enough,' said the giant fly.

'They ought to,' said Frank.

'They don't get enough money to buy more food,' said the giant fly.

'They ought to,' said Frank

'Mr Bryman won't give them any more,' said the giant fly.

'He gave some to the museum,' said Frank.

'We know that,' said the giant fly.

'They shouldn't work for him,' said Frank.

'There's nowhere else to work,' said the giant fly.

'How am I going to get Mum out of there?' said Frank.

'You'll have to do it yourself,' said the giant fly. 'You'll have to work it out for yourself. We can't help you.'

'We can't help you,' said the plastic skeleton, 'we're just plastic exhibits.'

So Frank sat down in front of the big white statue and began to think.

Chapter Ten

FRANK SAT AND THOUGHT.

'I can't do this on my own. I can't do it with the giant fly. I can't do it with the plastic skeleton. Who else can help me?'

He thought of all the other people he had met. Space suit? The stone men? Tiger? He couldn't see how any of them could help. Then as he sat there, his eyes landed on the plaque underneath the statue and he saw the name Sybil Longstone. He remembered her standing high up on the gangplank telling off the stone men. Maybe she could help. In fact he was sure she could help. He got up.

'I want to see Mrs Longstone,' said Frank.

'No,' said the giant fly, 'you can't.'

'I've seen her already,' said Frank.

'But that's because she saw you,' said the plastic skeleton.

'You can't go and see her,' said the giant fly.

'Where is she?' said Frank.

'We know where she is,' said the plastic skeleton, 'but you mustn't go in. It's not allowed.'

'Why not?' said Frank.

'No one knows why it's not allowed. It's a secret,'

said the plastic skeleton.

'Why is it a secret?' said Frank.

'If we knew why it was a secret, it wouldn't be a secret any more, would it?' said the giant fly.

'Show me where she is,' said Frank.

'If you go in, the most awful and terrible things will happen.'

'Like what?' said Frank.

'We don't know,' said the plastic skeleton, 'because no one's ever gone in.'

'How do you know awful things will happen?' said Frank.

'Because the man who started the museum said so,' said the plastic skeleton 'and he must know.'

'Who started the museum?' said Frank. 'Mr Longstone, of course.'

Frank looked at the plaque. 'Herbert and Sybil Longstone.' He reckoned Sybil Longstone must know a thing or two, though he didn't much like what he'd seen of her so far. Never mind, he thought, I've got to see her or I'll never get Mum out of there.

So he said to the others, 'Take me to see where she is.'

They were worried.

The giant fly kept saying, 'Oh dear, oh dear, oh dear.'

And the plastic skeleton was saying, 'This is dangerous. This is really dangerous. Oh pickled onions, pickled onions. If only I had known. The whole place is pickled onions, not doughnuts.'

'Take me to see Mrs Longstone,' said Frank very firmly.

'So the giant fly and the plastic skeleton led Frank off along a corridor, up some stairs, along another corridor, up some more stairs until they got to a dark little door marked PRIVATE, NO ENTRY.

'She's there,' said the giant fly.

'Right,' said Frank, 'I'm going in, are you com-ing?'

'No,' said the plastic skeleton.

'Not me,' said the giant fly.

So Frank opened the door.

Straight in front of him was another door. On this door was the sign: EVEN MORE PRIVATE. NO ENTRY AT ALL. Frank opened this door and the one behind him shut. Straight in front of him was another door. On this door was a sign, it said: UNBELIEVABLY PRIVATE: INCREDIBLY NO CHANCE OF ENTRY. Frank opened this door and immediately he heard shouting. Two people were shouting at each other. One was a woman, one was a man. Frank was in a small dark room. It was piled high with wooden carvings, statues, figures of heads, faces, masks and animals. They were all looking at Frank. Some of them stared. Some of them looked as if they were laughing, some of them were grinning, some of them looked angry, some of them looked sad.

The noise of the shouting was coming from another room, through another door. On this door there was one of those signs that say KNOCK AND ENTER, except someone had written on it. Now it said: DON'T KNOCK AND DON'T ENTER.

The woman's voice is Mrs Longstone, thought Frank.

She said, 'You're a nimcompoop, you're a buffoon, you're a damnable idiot.'

The man's voice said, 'I don't have to put up with this from you, woman. This is my museum.'

Mrs Longstone said, 'It's not your museum. If it's anyone's museum it's Joseph Bryman's and General Fawcett's.

'Oh no it isn't,' said the man. 'It's mine, mine, mine. I may have things to thank those two men for but it's my museum.'

'Pickled onions,' said Mrs Longstone.

'Pickle yourself,' said the man.

'And I'll tell you something else, Herbert Longstone,' said Mrs Longstone, 'If I'm alive after you, the day you die, General Fawcett goes out of this museum.'

'You dare, you dare,' said Mr Longstone, 'I'll write it down in my will. That the statue can never, never, never be moved.'

'I'll throw it out, you old lunatic.'

'Then every piece of General Fawcett's treasure will curse you for the rest of your days, woman.'

'It isn't Fawcett's treasure. It's the African's trea-

73

sure.'

Frank thought he had had enough. He stepped up to the door and opened it.

He was in an old room, piled high with papers and knick‑knacks, ornaments, old clocks, pictures all over the walls, mantlepieces and window sills piled high with bowls, and carvings, and plates and things.

Mr Longstone was sitting at a desk and Mrs Longstone was pacing to and fro in the room.

'I want my mum,' said Frank.

Mr and Mrs Longstone looked round. Mrs Long‑stone was still wearing that long black dress, and Mr Longstone had on a black suit.

Mrs Longstone said, 'How dare you? How dare you, boy? Don't you know? No one is allowed in here. No one at all.'

'Why not?' said Frank.

'Because we don't want people to hear us shouting at each other,' said Mr and Mrs Longstone together at the same time.

'It's a secret,' they said.

'It's not a secret any more, is it?' said Frank.

'No,' they said.

'I want my mum,' said Frank.

'Where is she?' they said.

'In Bryman's pickles factory,' said Frank.

'Well you can't have her,' they said. 'If she's not making pickles, Joseph Bryman can't sell his pickles, he won't get any money and so we won't get any

74

either,' they said.

'Well I'm going to get her out of there,' said Frank. 'I'm going to go downstairs, I'm going to open up his big fat chest, and I'm just going to pull her out.'

'You can't, you can't. It's our museum. You can't,' they said.

'I am,' said Frank. 'I'm going to pull her out. I'm going to pull them all out.'

'You can't bring that lot into our museum,' they said.

'I will,' said Frank.

'You haven't got anywhere to put them,' they said. 'You haven't got a glass case. Everything has to have a glass case. You can't put something in the museum if you haven't got a glass case.'

As they were saying this, Mr Longstone was moving towards Frank. 'We've got the glass cases. We decide what goes in the glass cases,' he said.

Frank noticed that Mr Longstone was making signs to Mrs Longstone. She opened an old glass case that was standing on the floor. It had a new sign on it: FRANK.

Mr Longstone got nearer.

Mrs Longstone started pushing the glass case towards Frank as well. Frank looked in the case. It was big enough for him to be put in. It got nearer and nearer. Mr Longstone was reaching out towards him. His hands touched Frank. The door of the glass case was open and waiting for him.

Frank shouted: 'Oh no you don't. Oh no you don't,' and he gave Mr Longstone a great big push.

Mr Longstone staggered backwards and tripped. He fell straight into the glass case. The case fell back on to the floor. As it landed with a bang, the door slammed shut tight. There was Mr Longstone lying on his back looking up out of a glass case on the floor. He wasn't moving. He just lay there staring up at Frank and Mrs Longstone.

Mrs Longstone stood staring down at him. She was frozen to the spot. She didn't move, she didn't breathe. She was rooted to the ground.

'I'm going to get my mum,' said Frank, and he turned round, walked through the door, past the heads and masks and faces, through the doors and back to where the giant fly and the plastic skeleton were waiting for him.

'Hallo,' said Frank.

'Well, well, well,' said the giant fly. 'I didn't think I'd see you come out of there alive.'

'How did you think I'd come out?' said Frank.

'Dead,' said the giant fly.

'Dead in a glass case,' said the plastic skeleton

'You mean you knew,' said Frank.

'Yes,' said the giant fly.

'Yes,' said the plastic skeleton.

'Well I'm blowed,' said Frank.

Chapter Eleven

'I HAVEN'T GOT much time left, I have to get back to my glass case,' said the plastic skeleton. 'We must hurry.'

'Come on then,' said Frank.

'But we haven't found the real wild man's skeleton yet.'

But Frank was off down the corridor already.

'Plenty of real *flies* about, though, aren't there?' said the giant fly. 'So I don't have to go looking for any of them.'

And they hurried off after Frank back to the glass house.

When they got there, Frank was already at the statue opening up the door.

He knew what to do. Just pull his mother out of Joseph Bryman's chest. He tried . . . but he couldn't. No matter how hard he tried, he just couldn't do it on his own. He looked at the other two. Plastic skeleton was getting cross. He wanted to get on with looking for the real wild man. Giant fly was looking for real flies now that he remembered that there were real flies in the world. He was going up to them and talking to them. 'Hallo little fly,' he said. They didn't seem very interested in talking to him though. Who could he get to help him? Mrs Longstone had been no good.

'I know,' he said, 'Tiger!'

'Back in a minute,' said Frank, and away he ran to the stairs. 'Tiger, Tiger, help me, I know where my mum is, I know what I've got to do, but I can't do it.'

Tiger didn't say anything, but got off her stand and followed Frank back to the glass house.

'She's in there,' said Frank, and he pointed to the place in Bryman's chest.

Tiger climbed up and looked in. 'It's a bit like the elephants,' said Tiger.

'It's nothing like elephants,' said Frank.

'Listen,' said Tiger, 'those elephants that came to kill me should have said, "We're fed up with being spiked in the back. We've got nothing against tigers and tigers have got nothing against us. We don't need to do this job of hunting tigers. It's tiring us out, it's killing beautiful tigers and it's killing us. All we need to do is dump these men off our backs and go back to eating leaves and leaving tigers alone." That's what those elephants should have done,' said Tiger, 'and then I wouldn't be here now, would I?'

'I want to get Mum out of there,' said Frank, 'and you're not helping me.'

'Look,' said Tiger, 'they couldn't go off and eat leaves because they thought they had to go on hunting tigers for those people. Now work the rest out yourself.'

At that, Tiger turned tail and loped off back to her place on the stairs.

'All the elephants needed to do,' thought Frank 'was stop it . . . but they *thought* they had to go on hunting tigers for those people . . . is that what Tiger meant? . . . That's it. Bryman's got her trapped in there because she *thinks* she has to go on making pickles for him. I can't get her out until she stops thinking that. Making pickles for Bryman is like hunting tigers for King George the Fifth. That's it.'

Frank stepped up to the statue, he opened up the door in the chest and yelled at the top of his voice, 'STOPPIT STOPPIT. MAKING PICKLES IS LIKE HUNTING TIGERS.'

No one seemed to take any notice. The women went on doing the cutting and chopping and pouring. They still seemed so tired and so old. But then as he watched, he noticed something. When the man who walked up and down had his back turned, one woman spoke to another woman. Then another woman spoke to another woman – just a quick whisper, it was, when his back was turned. And so it went on round all the women until every single one of them had heard whatever it was that was being said. It all happened so quickly, like a breath of wind passing over grass.

Then one woman spoke out loud to the woman next to her. 'Your hair's come down at the back, love.'

Up jumped the man. 'Right, Palmer, that's you done for. You'll have money to pay for this *and* Mr Bryman to see.'

At that, all the women simply stopped doing what they were doing. Every single one of them stopped in the middle of their chopping and pouring. The man stepped forwards and grabbed Frank's mum. No sooner had he done that than all the other women moved in together and grabbed the man. They pulled him off Frank's mum, they picked him up struggling and kicking and swearing and carried him as fast as they could through the low dark room up to a giant vat of vinegar that was sitting at one end. There was a moment's pause. And then, with one great heave, they threw him into the vinegar vat.

'That's you pickled,' said one.

'Now what?' thought Frank.

But as he stood there, he heard a cracking noise, and he realized that just a few inches away from his nose, Joseph Bryman was falling apart. The front fell off his chest. Another crack and the head fell off.

The giant fly looked up from catching flies and said to the plastic skeleton, 'Bryman's head isn't very real either. You're not the only one, you know.'

But Frank was looking into Bryman's empty body. The factory was now sitting there just where Frank could reach it. All he had to do was put his hands in and lift it out.

It came out like a doll's house. He stood there with

it in his hands. But then, because he wasn't holding
on to anything, he lost his balance, he teetered backwards and started to fall. The factory went up in the
air. 'Catch!' screamed Frank as he toppled backwards off the statue on to the floor. The plastic skeleton leapt forwards and just caught it. Frank crashed
to the floor, but as he did so, one of the figures of one

of the women flew out through the door of the factory and fell on the floor beside Frank.

Frank went to pick it up. It was his mum. She was about as big as his hand, her arms were still yellow and her skin was still looking as if it was about to peel. She was standing there, tired and shivering.

'Hallo, Mum,' said Frank.

'Hallo Frank,' said Mum.

The plastic skeleton put the Joseph Bryman's pickle factory between Joseph Bryman's legs.

'Huh,' said the giant fly, 'good place to leave it. Then everyone who sees the statue will see the pickles at the same time.'

'And us,' said Frank's mum.

'You're a bit small, Mum,' said Frank.

'That's you, isn't it? Moan, moan moan. I'm your mum, aren't I?'

'I hope so,' said Frank, but he had to admit it, he was a bit disappointed.

'Right,' said the plastic skeleton. 'Now to find the real wild man's skeleton. Are you coming?'

'Coming where?' said Frank.

'Er . . . I don't know,' said the plastic skeleton.

'It'll be difficult to find the real wild man's skeleton if we don't know where to look,' said the giant fly.

'I know,' said Frank, 'back to the Longstones. Are you coming, Mum?'

'I can't keep up with you, you'll have to carry me.'

'OK,' said Frank.

Just then they heard a cough. They looked round. It was General Fawcett. Frank had forgotten all about him standing there. He coughed again.

'Oh no,' said the giant fly, 'what's woken him up?'

'Pickled onions,' said Mum.

'But we haven't got any pickled onions,' said Frank.

'Yes we have,' said the giant fly, 'smell that,' and he pushed Frank towards the factory between Joseph Bryman's feet.

And sure enough, the smell of pickles and pickled onions was pouring out of the little factory.

General Fawcett coughed again. 'He loves pickled onions,' said Mum.

'How do you know?' said Frank.

'Because General Fawcett got the army to buy thousands of jars of pickles from Bryman for his army in Africa.'

The giant fly was standing looking from Bryman to Fawcett and back to Bryman again, saying: '*He* made the pickles, *he* bought the pickles, *he* made the pickles, *he* bought the pickles.'

'No,' said Mum, '*we* made the pickles.'

'Right,' said the giant fly, '*you* made the pickles, but Bryman got the money. Bryman got the money when Fawcett bought the pickles. Then the Long-stones got the money *and* they got the treasure. Well, well, well.'

General Fawcett suddenly spoke. He had a loud

fruity voice. 'I can see you're not wearing the right trousers.'

The giant fly said, 'I don't wear trousers.'

The plastic skeleton said, 'I don't wear trousers.'

Mum said, 'I don't wear trousers.'

Frank said, 'What are the right trousers?'

General Fawcett said, 'Do you know what the Union Jack is, boy?'

Frank said, 'I thought we were talking about trousers.'

'The trousers you should be wearing today, boy,' said General Fawcett, 'are Union Jack trousers. They're in the drawer down below.'

Frank pulled out the drawer and took out a pair of trousers made of the Union Jack flag.

'Why does he have to put them on today?' said Mum.

'Because today,' said General Fawcett? 'is The Day of The Wheel Falling Off General Fawcett's Gun Carriage, one hundred and twenty-two years ago today.'

After General Fawcett said that, there was a sound of bugles going Tarantaraaaa Tarantaraaaa Tarantaraaaa and a wheel rolled out of the wall next to the statue.

'That is the wheel that fell off my gun carriage, boy,' said General Fawcett. 'Now put the trousers on. The wheel will be shown on television next week and then the whole country will put on Union Jack trousers.'

'I don't want to wear Union Jack trousers,' said Mum.

'Nor do I,' said the Giant Fly.

'I don't either,' said the plastic skeleton.

'You wait,' roared General Fawcett. 'When you watch the television showing of The Day of The Wheel Falling Off General Fawcett's Gun Carriage, you will.'

Frank was looking at the wheel. He noticed that it was dirty. Well, it was sort of stained anyway. He pointed it out to the plastic skeleton.

'It's dirty,' said Frank.

'It's not dirt,' said the plastic skeleton, 'It's blood.'

'What blood?' said Frank.

'The blood he got the medals for, remember them?' said the plastic skeleton.

'And the pickled onions,' said Mum.

'Wear the trousers,' said General Fawcett.

'No thanks,' said Frank.

'Come on,' said the plastic skeleton, 'I've had enough of this. I want to find the real wild man and I've scarcely got enough time left.'

Frank dropped the trousers on the floor and then stopped for a moment to look at them.

Chapter Twelve

'Come on,' said the plastic skeleton', 'let's go, let's go.'

'Where *is* General Fawcett's treasure?' said Frank.

'Can't stop now,' said the plastic skeleton. So, without any more hanging about, they all dashed off up the corridor towards the Longstones.

The plastic skeleton in the lead, shouting, 'Now for the real wild man, now for the real wild man, oh pickled pickled onions, pickled pickled onions.'

They all arrived at the door marked Private more or less together, the plastic skeleton, the giant fly, Frank and his mother in his hand.

'We're going in,' said the plastic skeleton.

Through the doors they went, past the wooden faces and heads and masks.

'That's General Fawcett's treasure,' said the giant fly. 'That's the stuff the Nigerians want back.'

'What's it doing here?' said Frank.

'Can't stop now,' said the plastic skeleton and they rushed on into the Longstone's room.

There stood Mrs Longstone, exactly as Frank had left her, standing frozen to the floor, staring down at

Mr Longstone lying in the glass case stretched out on the floor. They hadn't moved.

'Oh, that's hopeless,' said the plastic skeleton. 'I can't ask them now. Look at them. I'll never find out where he is now. I'll never find the real wild man. This whole thing has been a waste of time. And it's your fault, boy. If you hadn't come in here and frozen them I could have found out.'

'But you said that it was too dangerous to come in here yourself,' said Frank.

'Shuttup,' said the plastic skeleton.

The giant fly had an idea. 'Let's look through their books and papers.'

'Can I have a rest?' said Mum.

The plastic skeleton and the giant fly went over to the desk and the drawers and began a long search through everything. Books flew in all directions, drawers were tipped up, pieces of paper fell to the floor, cups were knocked over, ink was spilt.

Frank sat with Mum in his hand and watched.

Every now and then the giant fly or the plastic skeleton would grunt or mutter or say, 'Ahaaa' or 'Mmmmm', but nothing much until, suddenly, the plastic skeleton stood up with a bit of paper in his hand and screamed. He screamed and screamed 'Ahhhhhhhhhhhhhhhhhhhhhhhhhhhhhhhhhhhh.' As he screamed Frank ran over to him and looked at the piece of paper in his hand. On it was written:

The Wild Man of Ashton Forest

The skeleton of the wild man of Ashton Forest is in fact the skeleton of John Straw, a lunatic. There never was a wild man of Ashton Forest. Many deaths, bad weather, floods and illnesses were blamed on the 'wild man'. John Straw never lived anywhere near Ashton Forest. His skeleton was given to the museum by the warden of Greytowers Asylum.

All this was written in old handwriting, the date was 1879 and there was someone's name there too: Herbert Longstone. Underneath it was written, 'We have made a plastic copy, and buried the John Straw skeleton in Greytowers cemetery. This very popular exhibit can stay on show for a while longer.' This was stamped 'City Museum' but there was no date.

The plastic skeleton went on screaming: 'Ahhh-hhhhhhhhhhhhh, I'm Not Real, I'm Not Real.'

As he screamed on and on, Frank saw him very slowly crumple, shrink, collapse and slowly turn to dust in front of his eyes. Then with him went the giant fly, crumbling, shrinking, breaking down, down into dust, and then the Longstones too, their room, the walls, the doors with their signs on, even his mother in his hand; they all crumbled to dust in front of his eyes, crumbling, crumbling, crumbling, until all he could see was a haze of dust.

All that was left was Frank himself and General

Fawcett's treasure.

The faces and the masks looked at Frank. One of the great wooden heads had big dark eyes that stared at him. Frank stared back into the deep dark eyes and slowly but surely into those eyes, all the people he had met began to appear; one after another they came into view: the plastic skeleton, the stone men, Space Suit, Tiger, The Bartlett Collection, Elvis Presley, Marilyn Monroe, the giant fly, Embryo, the Longstones, Joseph Bryman, the pickle factory women, General Fawcett and his tiny, tiny mum.

Then bit by bit, just as all the people had appeared in the big dark eye, they now disappeared. All except for Mum. She was the last. Frank stared at her standing in the dark eye.

As Frank stared at her, it seemed to him that she was getting nearer and nearer and nearer. And as she got nearer, she was getting bigger and bigger until suddenly there she was standing over him.

She spoke to him: 'That's it. My job done for another week. Come on, you. Home!'

Frank got up, picked up his comic and followed Mum to the side door. As he followed her, he had to walk past the glass cases. The first one he recognized was the one full of the bowls and jugs that the stone men were going to throw at him.

'It's going back to Nigeria,' said Frank.

'So's your Uncle Charlie,' said Mum.

'But I haven't got an Uncle Charlie,' said Frank.

'Well, he's not going back to Nigeria then is he, son?' said Mum.

A few seconds later they passed by the glass case of the plastic skeleton of the wild man of Ashton Forest. There it stood. Absolutely still.

There was the sign:

'For years the wild man roamed through Ashton Forest terrifying children, threatening farmers and killing cattle, until finally it died in 1886. This is a plastic copy of the original skeleton.'

'Rubbish,' said Frank. 'That's rubbish.'

'Don't talk about things you know nothing about,' said Mum. 'Come on, now.'

And Mum and Frank walked out of the museun into the night.

All About Barn Owl Books

If you've ever scoured the bookshops for that book you loved as a child or the one your children wanted to hear again and again and been frustrated then you'll know why Barn Owl Books exists. We are hoping to bring back many of the excellent books that have slipped from publishers' backlists in the last few years.

Barn Owl is devoted entirely to reprinting worthwhile out-of-print children's books. Initially we will not be doing any picture books, purely because of the high costs involved, but any other kind of children's book will be considered. We are always on the lookout for new titles and hope that the public will help by letting us know what their own special favourites are. If anyone would like to photocopy and fill in the form below and give us their suggestions for future titles we would be delighted.

We do hope that you enjoyed this book and will read our other Barn Owl titles.

Books I would like to see back in print include:

_____

_____

_____

_____

Signature

_____

Address

_____

_____

Please return to Ann Jungman, Barn Owl Books
15 New Cavendish Street, London W1M 7AL

Barn Owl Books

THE PUBLISHING HOUSE DEVOTED ENTIRELY TO
THE REPRINTING OF CHILDREN'S BOOKS

TITLES AUTUMN 1999

Jimmy Jelly – Jacqueline Wilson

Angela just loves Jimmy Jelly when she sees him on tv. It's a bit different when
she meets him in the flesh. A charming story for first readers. (£3.99)

Private – Keep Out! – Gwen Grant

The hilarious story of a family growing up immediately after the war.
Told by the anarchic and rebellious diary-keeping youngest sister . . . it is ideal
for confident readers. (£4.99)

You're thinking about doughnuts – Michael Rosen

When Frank is left alone in the museum, while his mother does the cleaning,
he doesn't expect the skeleton to come alive and introduce him to the exhibits.
A gripping read for the confident reader. (£4.99)

Voyage – Adèle Geras

The story of a group of migrants leaving Russia for the USA in 1905.
During the weeks at sea, hopes and fears surface and love is explored as they wait
for the great adventure in the New World to begin.
Suitable for teenagers. (£4.99)

TITLES PLANNED FOR 2000

The Mustang Machine – Chris Powling

Your guess is as good as mine – Bernard Ashley

Hairs in the palm of the hand – Jan Mark

The Little Dragon Steps Out – Ann Jungman